CH

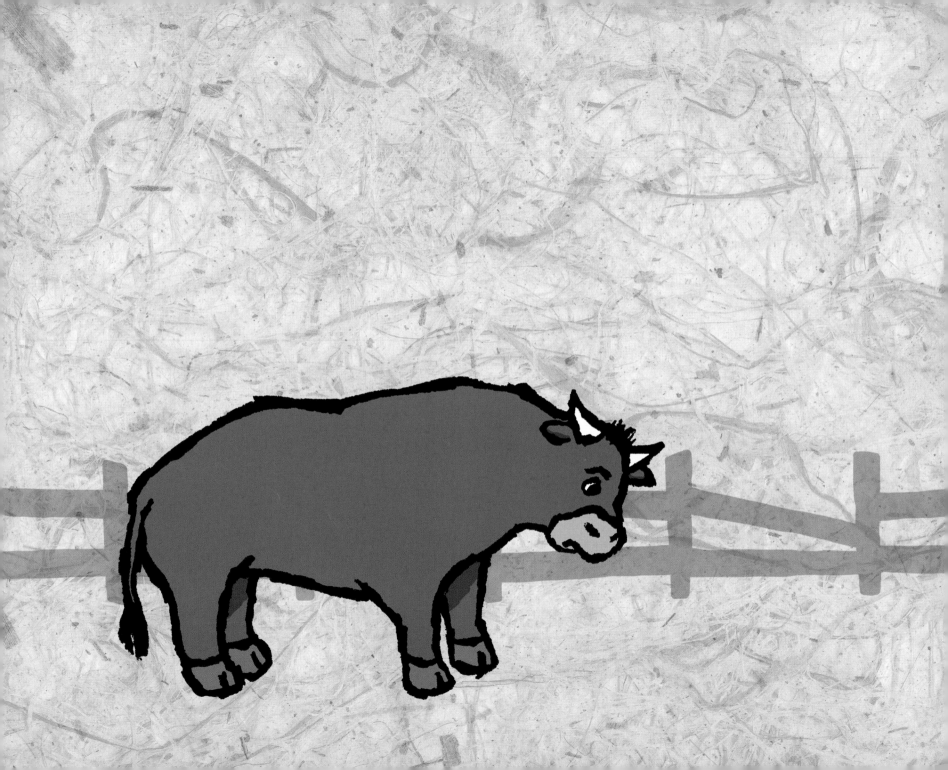

BULLY

Laura Vaccaro Seeger

A NEAL PORTER BOOK

ROARING BROOK PRESS

NEW YORK

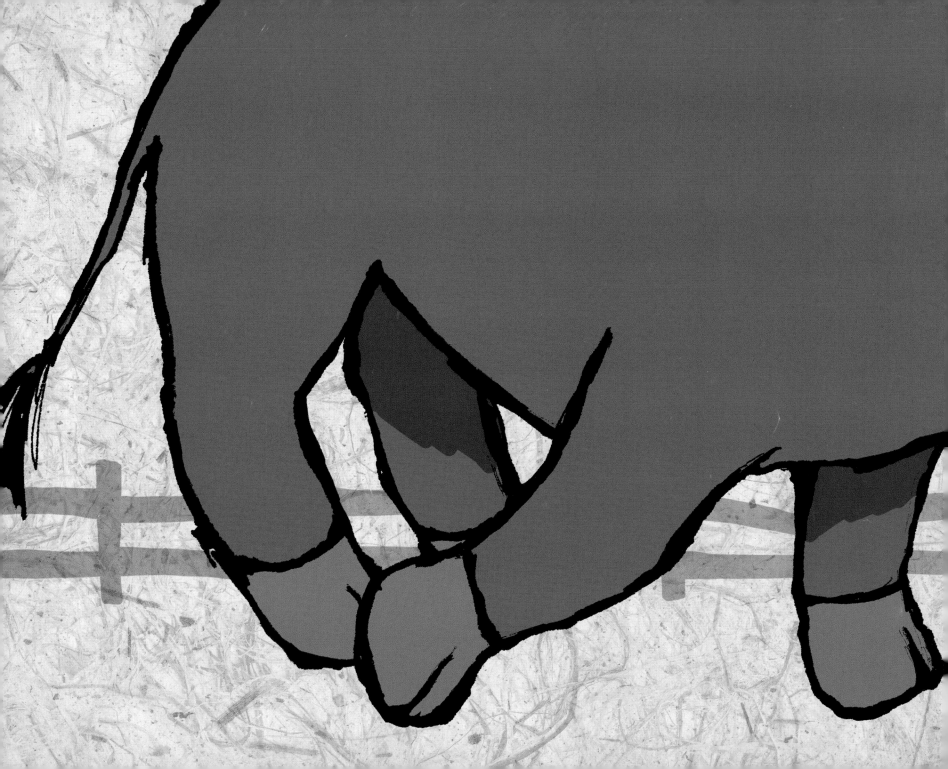

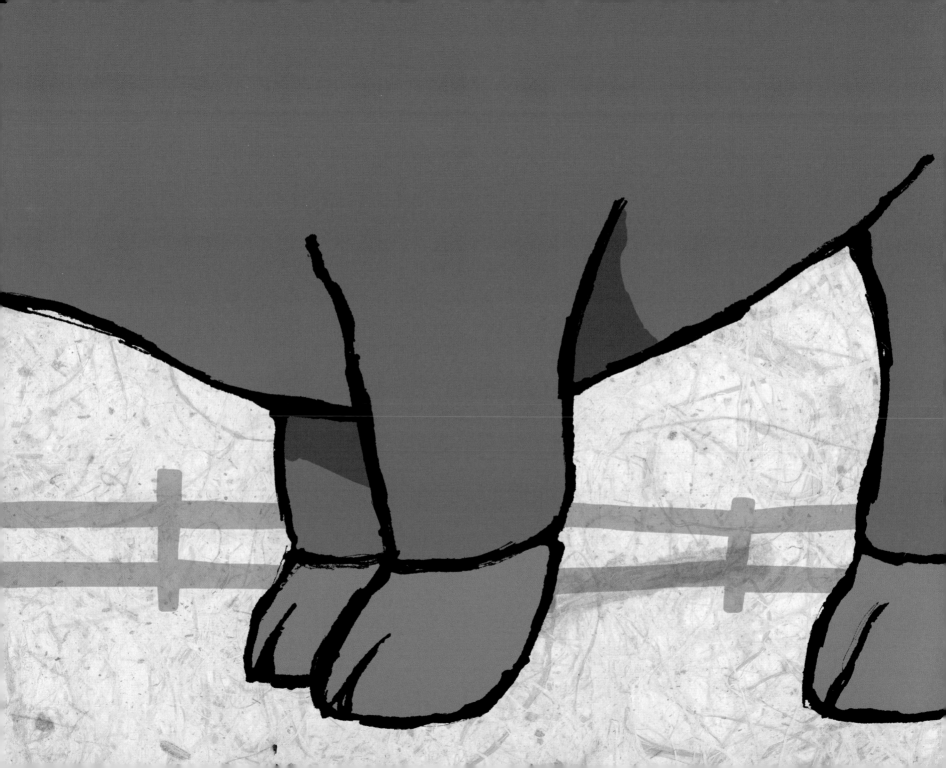

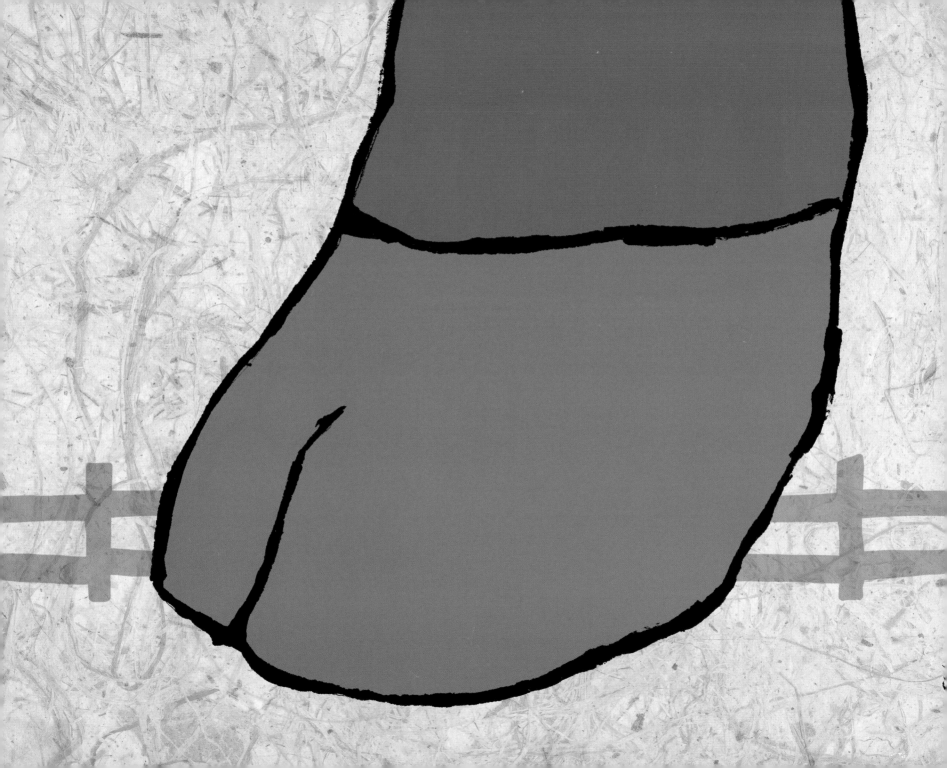

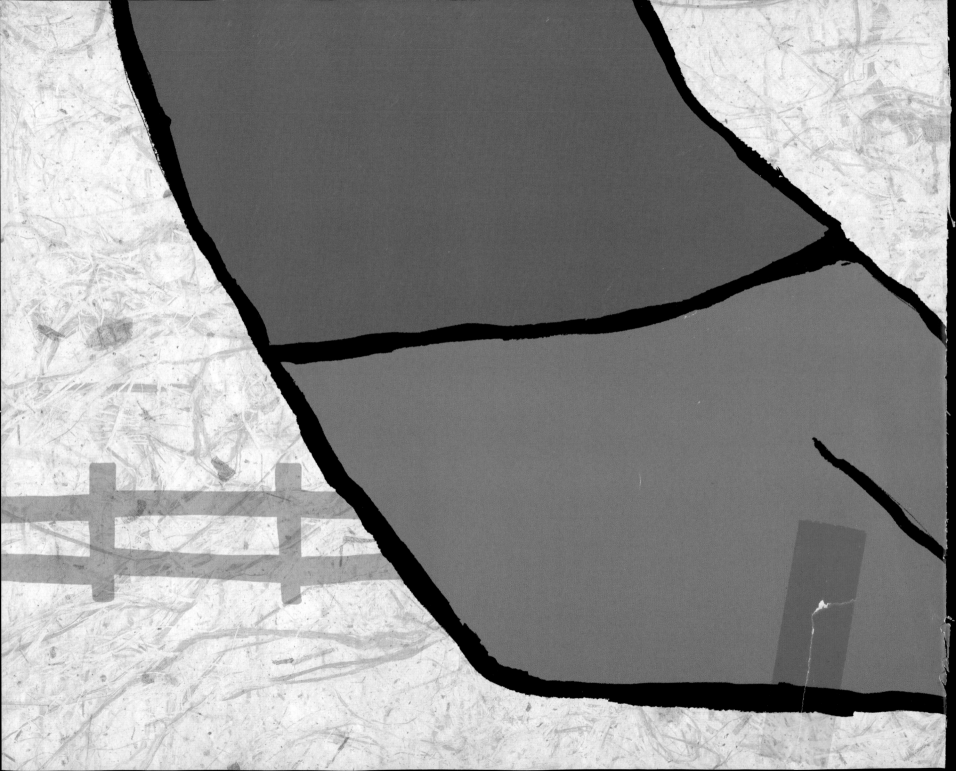

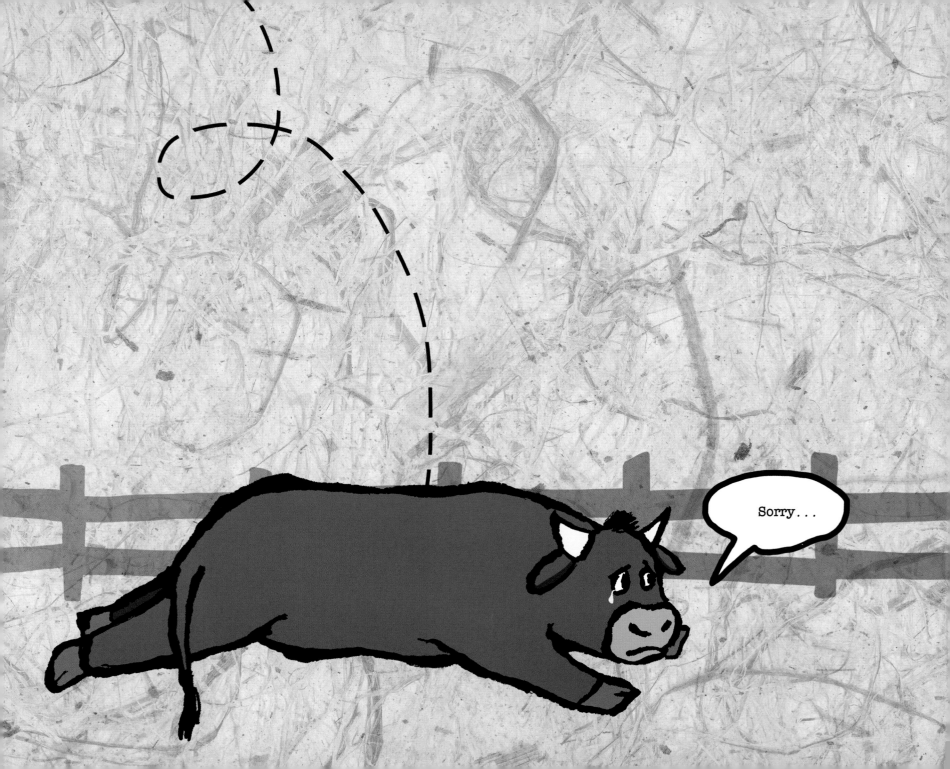

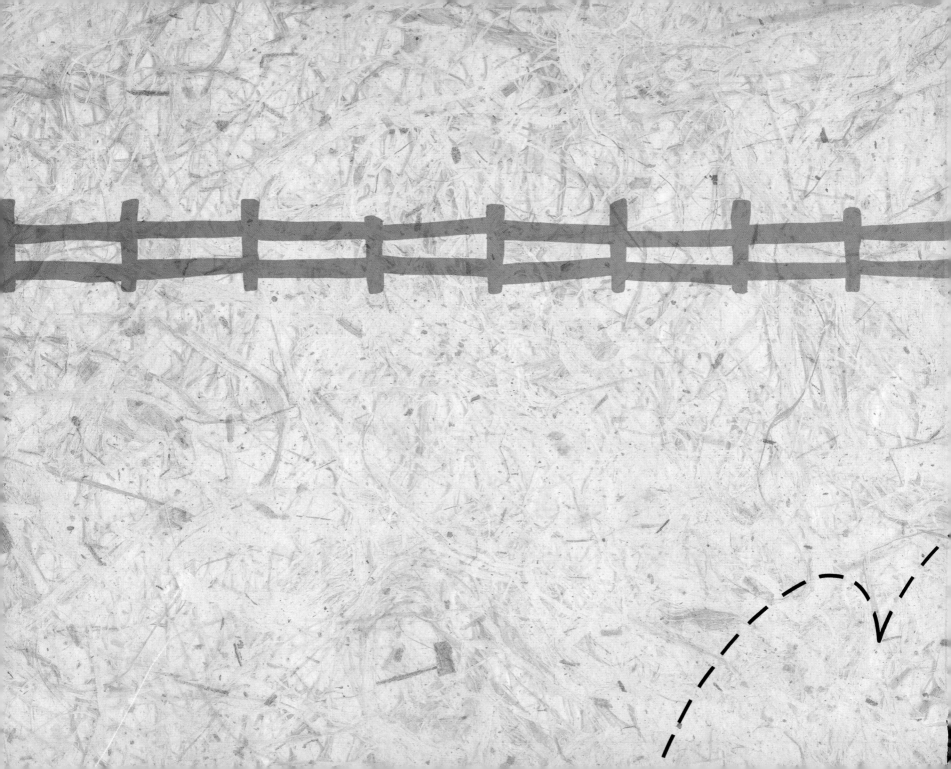

for my niece and nephews,
Laura, Will, Keith, and Philip

Copyright © 2013 by Laura Vaccaro Seeger

A Neal Porter Book

Published by Roaring Brook Press

Roaring Brook Press is a division of Holtzbrinck Publishing Holdings Limited Partnership

175 Fifth Avenue, New York, New York 10010

mackids.com

Library of Congress Cataloging-in-Publication Data

Seeger, Laura Vaccaro.

Bully / Laura Vaccaro Seeger. — 1st ed.

　　p. cm.

"A Neal Porter Book."

Summary: A little bull discovers that he has been a big bully.

ISBN 978-1-59643-630-5 (hardcover)

[1. Bullies—Fiction. 2. Bulls—Fiction. 3. Domestic animals—Fiction.]

I. Title.

　　PZ7.S4514Bul 2013

　　[E]—dc23

2012012991

Roaring Brook Press books are available for special promotions and premiums.

For details contact: Director of Special Markets, Holtzbrinck Publishers.

First edition 2013

Printed in China by Toppan Leefung Printing Ltd., Dongguan City, Guangdong Province

1　3　5　7　9　10　8　6　4　2